MW01268117

SCIENCE ENCOUNTERS

Sports

JULIAN ROWE

RIGBY
INTERACTIVE
LIBRARY

Interiors designed by **AMR**
Illustrations by Art Construction
Printed in the United Kingdom

00 99 98 97 96
10 9 8 7 6 5 4 3 2 1

Library of Congress Cataloging-in-Publication Data

Rowe, Julian.
    Sports / Julian Rowe.
        p.   cm. – (Science encounters)
Includes bibliographical references and index.
Summary: Examines the scientific principles and technological advances
important to participation in and coverage of such sports as track and field,
baseball, tennis, skiing, and football.
    ISBN 1-57572-089-2
    1. Physics–Juvenile literature. 2. Sports–Juvenile literature.
3. Force and energy–Juvenile literature. [1. Sports.2. Science.]
I. Title. II. Series.
Q163.R67   1997
688. 7'6–dc20   96-33351
                                                        CIP
                                                        AC

Acknowledgments
The publisher would like to thank the following for permission to reproduce photographs.
Action-Plus, p. 4, p. 5, p. 6, p. 7, p. 9, p. 24, p. 26, p. 27, p. 28, p. 29; Topham Picture Source, p. 8;
Allsport, p. 11, p. 12, p. 14, p. 17; Telegraph Colour Library, p. 16; Allsport USA, p. 20, p. 21, p. 23;
Science Photo Library, p. 22

Every effort has been made to contact copyright holders of any material reproduced in this book.
Any omissions will be rectified in subsequent printings if notice is given to the publisher.

CONTENTS

SCIENCE IN SPORTS

People play sports for fun, to win, to break records, and sometimes just to stay fit. There are many different kinds of sports, including ball games, track and field sports, water sports, winter sports, and combat and target sports, to name just a few. Some sports are mechanical, because they depend on special machines Some sports, such as bar-flying, are played just for fun.

Many sports have developed gradually over thousands of years. Archery, for example, started as a hunting skill. There are pictures of archers in 10,000-year-old cave paintings in Spain. Other sports date from more recent times. For example, basketball was invented in 1891 in Springfield, Massachusetts.

Sports science is a field that uses scientific ideas to improve and develop sports. Science can help athletes to train better and can help with the design of new sporting equipment. New records and new feats of endurance in sports occur all the time. Many are the direct result of scientific knowledge that is being applied to nearly every sport.

These people are bar-flying. Dressed in a Velcro suit, they jump from a small trampoline onto a Velcro-covered wall. As you can see, they stick on the wall wherever they land!

The Business of Sports

There is nothing quite like being in the crowd at a big game. You experience the noise and the excitement. But if the action is at the other end of the field, you just cannot see it clearly! Sports photographers and TV cameras take pictures that capture exciting sports moments. But just how do the cameras get close enough to the action so that everyone can see what's going on? This book will tell you.

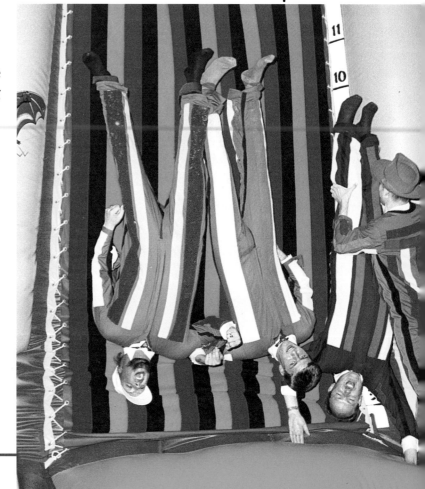

Sport is big business. The latest "high-tech" equipment allows athletes to shave hundredths of seconds off their times. Satellite television gives people around the world the chance to watch major sporting events. People's interest in sports and the skills and abilities of athlctes have never been greater. This book looks at the science behind some of the amazing feats athletes have achieved in their sports.

Sports Science in Action

As our scientific knowledge increases, the companies who make sporting equipment update the designs and the materials they use. Between 1910 and 1980, the world pole-vault record increased from 12.8 feet to 18.4 feet. Every 10 years, on average, it regularly increased by about 8 inches. However, between 1960 and 1970, the record shot up by 20 inches to 17.4 feet. What happened? Pole vaulters started to use a pole made of glass fiber. Athletes had experimented with **aluminum** and even bamboo poles, but **fiberglass** poles gave the best results. The current world record is more than 19 feet. The most current vaulting poles are made from **carbon fiber,** which is lightweight but springy and very strong. Now even more astonishing records may be achieved.

Here you can see just how much a vaulting pole can bend.

SPINNING BALLS

E very golfer has at some time sliced a ball and watched it spin off in the wrong direction. In baseball, a ball can leave the pitcher's hand spinning backward at 1,600 rpm (revolutions per minute). (When a car is not moving, its engine runs at about 800 rpm.) It covers the distance from the pitcher's mound to home plate (about 60 feet) in 0.4 seconds. The ball travels at 100 miles per hour and has time to spin only 10 or 11 times. The spin is enough to make the ball rise, or "hop" more than three inches in the air. Why do spinning balls swerve in the air?

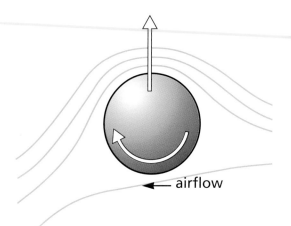

Magnus force

airflow

The pitcher can control Just how the ball spins as it flies through the air. The diagram shows how the air flowing around the spinning ball causes it to change direction.

The Spin Factor

In baseball, the pitcher's grip controls the way that the ball spins. The pitcher can make the ball swerve, float, or dip. As air passes over the top of a ball that is spinning backward, **friction** pulls some air part of the way around the back of the ball. This makes the trail left behind the ball in the air point downward. Because air passing over the ball has further to travel, it moves faster. This produces an area of low pressure above the ball. The higher pressure under the ball lifts it! This is called the Magnus effect, after Heinrich Gustav Magnus (1802–1870), a German professor of chemistry. It was he who described how a spinning ball experiences a sideways force.

Dimples

Long ago when golf balls were smooth, someone discovered, by accident, that a damaged golf ball flew through the air better than a smooth one. So now all golf balls have dimples. The record number of dimples in one ball is 552. The shape and size of the dimples are important, because they change the air flow around a ball in flight. Professional golfers want the balls they hit to have lots of spin, because this helps to control the ball's direction.

Today, more than 1 billion golf balls are made each year. Each one is made to an exact weight (not more than 1.75 ounces) and diameter (not less than 1.68 inches). Golf balls that are designed to travel further are not allowed in competitions—the courses would be too small!

A HAT FULL OF FEATHERS

The first golf balls were made of wood. They were replaced by balls made from a "top-hat full" of boiled feathers. The feathers were stitched into three pieces of leather. As the ball dried, the feathers expanded and the leather shrank. Craftspeople could only make four balls a day. For 250 years this is how golf balls were made!

RACKETS AND STRINGS

What do tennis rackets and airplanes have in common? They both are made from the same materials, which were developed for the aerospace industry. The first rackets with strings date from the 15th century and were made of wood. The frames were pear-shaped and not very strong, so their strings were only loosely strung. Modern rackets, like those now used in badminton, tennis, and squash, are made by combining different materials. Each material has its own special characteristics. What makes the rackets so strong and light?

Strong Nylon Strings

Plastics such as nylon are called **polymers.** They are made up of long **molecules.** Each molecule is made from smaller, identical molecules joined end-to-end. Rope is made strong by winding together long strands of fibers. In the same way, a polymer is strong because it consists of long lengths of connected molecules.

At the turn of the century, even world tennis champions played with wooden rackets.

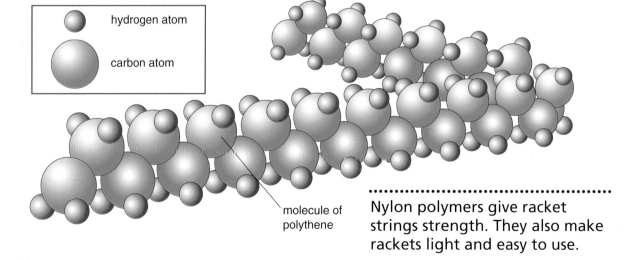

hydrogen atom

carbon atom

molecule of polythene

Nylon polymers give racket strings strength. They also make rackets light and easy to use.

Strong Rackets

Players tried metal tennis rackets in the 1920s. But then better wooden tennis rackets were developed. Their strong, light frames were made from thin strips of wood that were glued together. Professional players used these rackets until the 1970s.

Today's tennis racket frames are molded using a combination of strong, light materials such as fiberglass, graphite, and ceramics. Badminton, squash, and racquetball rackets are also constructed from these materials, which are known as composites. In fiberglass, for example, thin glass fibers are embedded in plastic to form a super-tough material. A tennis racket frame made only from fibers of glass would not last long!

Tough Strings

Synthetic, (artificially made) racket strings are made from as many as 48 separate plastic strands, called filaments. The strings are coated with a substance called silicone to protect them from water and dirt. A tennis racket can be very tightly strung with these strings. Taut (tight) strings spring backward and forward more evenly, allowing the player to control the ball better. A player can hear if a racket is correctly strung by striking the strings and listening to the note!

Strings made of natural gut, or animal insides, are still used in some rackets. They are more **elastic** than synthetic strings, and so they can be strung less tightly.

WHAT'S IN A NAME?

The name *tennis* comes from the game that was originally played in France. The server called "tenez," which means "hold" in French, to warn the other players that the game was about to begin.

Large-headed tennis rackets allow a player to control the ball better and also to hit it faster than ever.

FASTER THAN THE WIND

S ailboats can travel at very high speeds. A yacht at full speed sails at about 20 miles per hour. The record for an ice yacht is more than 140 miles per hour. Sand yachts have reached speeds of nearly 90 miles per hour, and sail boards regularly achieve speeds of more than 50 miles per hour. These speeds are much faster than the speed of the wind that fills the sails. How is this possible?

The Sail

The sail of a yacht is not just a bag that catches the wind. It is like the wing of an airplane standing on end. When air passes over an airplane wing it reduces the pressure of the air above it. The higher pressure below "lifts" the aircraft. Wind produces a similar difference in pressure across the curved sail of a yacht and, as a result, produces the force that drives the yacht forward. The blades of an ice yacht prevent it from drifting sideways, so all the wind's energy goes into pushing the yacht forward.

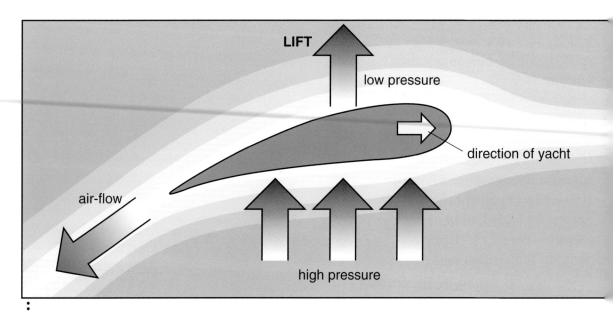

The curved, wind-filled sail of a yacht sailing at speed has much the same shape as the wing of an airplane.

Friction Brakes

Friction exists between any two surfaces that slide over one another. You can experience the force of friction by pushing your hand through water. A yacht has to overcome the force of friction between its hull (body) and the water. The smooth, sleek shape of the yacht's hull is designed to reduce friction. Ice yachts travel very fast, because there is very little friction between their blades and the ice.

Friction affects the performance of a sand yacht, too. Have you ever tried to ride a rusty old bicycle? You cannot turn the pedals, because friction prevents the wheels from moving around. When you oil the wheels they turn smoothly. Oil reduces friction, because it helps rough surfaces to slide over one another more easily. The wheels of a sand yacht have to be oiled as well.

SLIPPERY SHOES

Without friction, you would not be able to walk. Your shoes would slip on the pavement. When you walk on ice, friction is reduced. This is why it is so easy to slip.

WINDY WEATHER

Wind is caused by the sun's heat and the rotation of the earth. You can understand the amount of energy in wind when you see the massive damage caused by a tornado or a great storm. This wind energy is used, or captured, by the sails of a yacht. It also helps the giant propellers on "windmills" to make electricity.

Sand yachts can reach speeds of up to 90 miles per hour.

PEDAL POWER

Racing bicycles are built for speed. They have a strong but lightweight tubular frame. The placement of the handlebars allows the rider to be in a good position to turn the pedals easily. The large back wheel is driven by a chain through 12 or more gears. What do the gears on a bicycle do?

Gears

Gears help bicycle riders pedal more easily on steep slopes and flat surfaces. The bicycle chain runs around a group of **gear wheels,** called sprockets. These are attached to the back wheel. The biggest gear wheel probably has 30 teeth, the middle one has 23 teeth, and the smallest one has only 13 teeth. Look at the big sprocket gears that are attached to the pedals. The largest one has 46 teeth. Suppose the chain runs around the sprocket with 46 teeth and the one with 23 teeth. When you turn the pedals around once, the back wheel of the bicycle turns around twice. You are moving!

AS YOU STOP

When you are pedaling along energetically, both you and the bicycle are moving. Your body and the bicycle have a certain amount of energy called **kinetic energy**. But what happens to that energy when you brake and stop? Energy cannot be created or destroyed; it can only be changed from one form to another. Friction between the brake pads and the wheel rims converts the kinetic energy into heat. Brakes are a great device for converting kinetic energy into heat! The rider's energy is also converted into heat.

Shown here is a "high-tech" time-trial bicycle. When gripping its forward-pointing handlebars, the helmeted rider is in the best position for speed. Bikes like this one are designed for racing on indoor tracks.

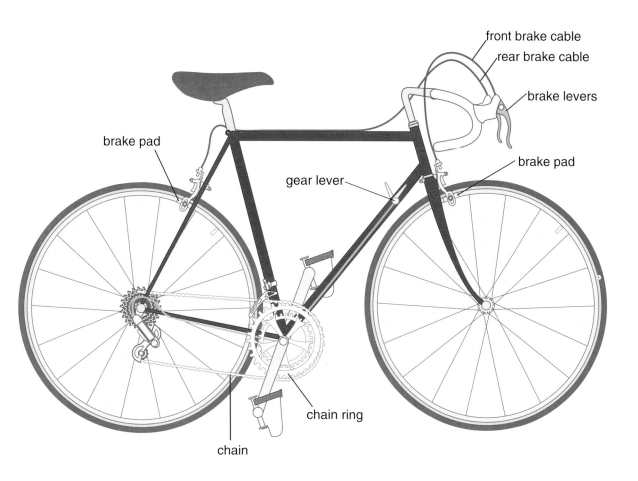

front brake cable
rear brake cable
brake levers
brake pad
brake pad
gear lever
chain ring
chain
brake pad

To change into a lower gear, you turn the gripshift. It is notched so that it clicks into the right place for the next gear. A lower gear means that you need to use much less effort. It is ideal for going uphill because it gives you greater **mechanical advantage.**

Cables in Control

When you turn the gripshift to change gear or pull on the brakes, you are using a lever to operate a cable control. The cable consists of a tough, steel wire that is threaded through a flexible metal tube. An outer plastic tube protects the metal one.

The brake lever is a simple lever that transmits (passes on) force in one direction only. The force is taken by cable to exactly where it is needed—where the brake pads press against the wheel rim.

SPEED ON SNOW

A speed skier races down a mountainside at more than 125 miles per hour. The record to beat is now 149 miles per hour. This is higher than the speed of a **free-fall** parachutist—before the parachute opens! Only 30 years ago, 60 miles per hour was considered fast for a downhill racer. How do today's skiers achieve such speed?

The Right Skis

Modern skis are specially designed for different purposes. Speed skis, which are designed to travel fast in straight lines, have to be long and stiff. Shorter and narrower **slalom** skis need to turn easily. Skis are made by combining layers of different materials into a mold. The layers are glued together. Fiberglass is used to give strength and stiffness, and **Kevlar** fibers add strength.

As a skier starts a run, adrenaline, the body chemical that speeds **reaction time,** rushes into the skier's bloodstream. The skier's heart rate reaches 200 beats per minute (at rest, the rate is about 70).

Smoother and Faster

The underside of a ski is made smooth with a coating of wax. The wax is put on while it's hot, and it binds to the outer layer of the skis. It can help a skier take a second or two off a downhill course. Protective headgear is designed to offer little air resistance.

Speedy Suits

A fast car is designed in such a way so it can travel with little disturbance to the flow of air around it. Any disturbance of the air, or **turbulence,** slows the car down. This is why ski suits are made from very smooth materials, just like the surface of a fast car or the hull of a yacht. They are designed to let the wearer slip through the air easily at high speeds.

Aluminum or plastic bindings attach the ski boots to the skis. They are adjusted for the skier's weight, age, ability, and foot size. To prevent injury, the bindings release automatically when a skier falls.

Foam-lined plastic boots with inflatable pads fit precisely around the skier's foot and ankle. They protect the skier from injury and help to control the skis.

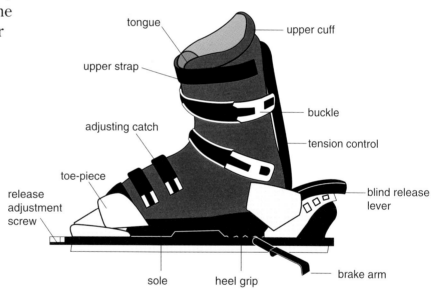

tongue
upper cuff
upper strap
buckle
adjusting catch
tension control
toe-piece
release adjustment screw
blind release lever
sole
heel grip
brake arm

SLED RACES AND MICROCHIPS

Sleds also go fast on snow and not just downhill! Each year in March, about 70 teams of 14 or more husky dogs pull aluminum and ash sleds in a 1,050-mile race from Anchorage to Nome on Alaska's Bering Strait. This 11-day race, called the Iditerod, is the biggest sporting event in Alaska. To prevent teams from changing their dogs during the race, each animal is tagged with a **microchip** placed under its skin.

SPECIAL SURFACES

Tennis courts, running tracks, soccer fields, and other kinds of sporting surfaces are made from a variety of different materials. Each type of surfacing material has advantages and disadvantages. For example, in sports such as soccer and tennis, most of the action takes place on one part of the field or court. The center of the soccer field and the penalty area wear out first, especially on a grass field. Most football fields are now covered with artificial grass instead of natural grass, and not all of them are green! What other sports benefit from artificial surfaces?

Rain or Shine

Older running tracks are made of grass, cinders, or tarmac. These surfaces wear away, because the lanes are used unevenly. Grass tracks become slippery when wet, but they can be used with most types of running shoe. Tarmac drains and dries easily, but athletes have to wear soft shoes on this surface. Cinders last for a long time, but they easily become waterlogged. Modern tracks are surfaced with tough rubber and plastic materials. They can be used for training and racing in all kinds of weather. They are designed to combine all the best features of the other types of surfaces.

This sports hall in Barcelona, Spain, was built especially for the 1992 Olympic Games. After it was built, games could be played in all types of weather.

Plastic Snow

Many skiers practice on artificial ski slopes, especially during warmer weather when there is no snow. The slopes are made of tufted (clustered together) nylon. They provide enough friction for skiers to practice their skills all year long. Without friction, the skiers would slide down the slopes out of control.

Grass or Clay?

Hard clay tennis courts allow the ball to bounce high and in a predictable way. This makes the game slower and easier for the players to control. On grass, the ball does not bounce as high, and is less predictable. So the game is very fast, and the outcome less certain!

SILENT RUNNING!

Several accidents took place on the running track during the 1976 Montreal Olympics. Some happened during distance events and were blamed on the fact that the artificial track was "silent." Runners simply could not hear others running close behind!

Climbers, too, can train all year around and without real mountains or rocks to climb. Walls constructed from plastic panels bolted to steel frames can be attached to the walls of halls or used as free-standing structures. Climbing centers in major cities now have 49-foot walls.

BEST FOOT FORWARD

Athletic shoes have come a long way from the first canvas shoes with rubber soles. Now you can buy shoes designed especially for your sport: running, football, tennis, basketball, baseball, and so on. Millions of pairs of athletic shoes are sold all around the world each year. How can a shoe help you to perform better?

Inflatable Shoes

Several shoe manufacturers have designed inflatable athletic shoes. A small air pump under the tongue of the shoe inflates a balloon-like airbag that surrounds the wearer's foot. This simple idea makes it possible to change the shoe design to suit different sports.

Inflatable shoes provide a perfect fit for athletes. They can also provide the right kind of support. Tennis players' feet, for example, need very different support around the ankle and under the foot compared to long-distance runners. This can be achieved very precisely by designing different shapes of inflatable airbags to fit inside the various types of athletic shoes.

In 1990, basketball players suddenly found they could jump higher when wearing a new kind of shoe. What made this shoe so special? It was inflatable.

A Spring to the Step

As athletes run, their feet pound the ground. Today's running shoes cushion the feet against these shocks by absorbing energy. Inside the middle of the sole of the shoe are built-in plastic tubes filled with air. As the midsole is squashed, the air inside these tubes **compresses.** This stores energy that "returns" to the athlete as the foot leaves the ground. As the plastic tubes spring back into shape, they push the athlete forward. This results in an improved and faster performance.

Springy Air

When you pump a bicycle tire, the air inside the pump is being compressed. You can feel just how "springy" this air is. This "springiness" is called elasticity. It is the way in which some materials return to their original shape after they have been squashed or stretched. Rubber, and some plastics, are very elastic. This elastic quality of compressed air together with the rubber like materials used to make modern athletic shoes combine to make these shoes better than ever before.

ADIDAS

In 1920 Adolf (Adi) and Rudolf Dassler began making the first specialized athletic shoes in a small town near Nuremberg, Germany. The brothers invented running spikes, studs for football boots, and screw-on spikes for mountaineers. They gave their name to the multinational sports manufacturer Adidas.

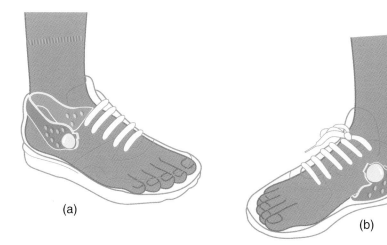

(a)

(b)

The **collar airbag (a)** holds the heel in the rear of the shoe and prevents it from lifting out. This is good for activities such as tennis or aerobics. The **arch airbag (b)** gives support to the instep or "arch" of the foot. This is important for long-distance runners.

SAFETY FIRST

In ice hockey, which is the fastest team game, players wear gloves, elbow pads, helmets, and chest, leg, and shoulder padding. Body armor like this is designed to absorb energy. Players of contact sports, such as football and baseball, also wear protective clothing. How do these important pieces of equipment prevent injury?

The Danger of Collisions

In billiards, you can see exactly how **momentum** is transferred when two balls collide. When a moving ball strikes one that is not moving head-on, the moving ball stops dead in its tracks, and the other one shoots forward. When you receive a blow to the side of your head, your brain moves, just like the shooting billiard. Your brain could be severely damaged as it collides with the inside of your skull.

Momentum

An object that is traveling along has momentum. Its momentum can be calculated by multiplying the weight of the moving object by the speed at which it is traveling. So a small, light object that is traveling very fast can have the same momentum as a heavy, slow-moving object. In a collision, the momentum of the moving object is transferred to whatever it strikes.

The first football helmets were made from boiled leather. Today's tough plastic helmets are fitted with unbreakable rubber-coated plastic face masks.

Ice-hockey players need gloves, elbow pads, helmets, and chest, leg, and shoulder padding. The goalie also wears a face mask.

Protective Clothing

So many football players were killed or injured in the early 1900s that rules about protective clothing were changed. Unlike a billiard ball, protective padding absorbs the energy transferred to it and then spreads it out. Inside football helmets are small containers, or cells, filled with air or liquid. This prevents injury by spreading evenly the effect of impact and slowing it down. Players even wear gum shields to protect their teeth. In addition to massive shoulder pads—some weigh 5.5 pounds—rib pads with a hard plastic shell protect the lower part of the body.

SCARY SPEEDS

The tough plastic helmet worn by baseball players has to withstand the impact of a baseball traveling at 90 miles per hour. In ice hockey, the goalies' "armor" has to protect them from a rubber puck traveling at 118 miles per hour!

SPORTS INJURIES

Many sports injuries are minor, like the muscle cramp sprinters get after a race. They do not cause any long-term damage to the athlete. Simple precautions, such as warming up properly, help to avoid pulled muscles. Muscles work better when they are 1° or 2°F above normal body temperature (98.6°F). Accidental injuries to muscles and bones have become accepted as a result of playing sports. What are some of the more common sports injuries?

Joint Damage

The ends of your knee bones, like the bones of other joints, are made of **cartilage.** This tissue is softer than the rest of the bone (which it protects from damage). Skaters, runners, jumpers, and other athletes sometimes tear the cartilage in their knees. As a result, the knee joint swells up, is painful, and may even lock in position. An operation to remove the damaged cartilage may cure the problem.

SWEATY WORK!

When you sweat your body cools down. This is because your body uses up 540 calories of energy in order to evaporate .035 ounces of water. Scientists use calories to measure how much energy foods give when they are used by the body. It is the loss of energy that cools the body! But as you sweat you lose salt. This is why sweat tastes salty! You need to replace this lost salt to keep your body fluids in balance. Otherwise your muscles may cramp and even collapse. An **isotonic drink** can help, because it has the same overall balance of salt as your body.

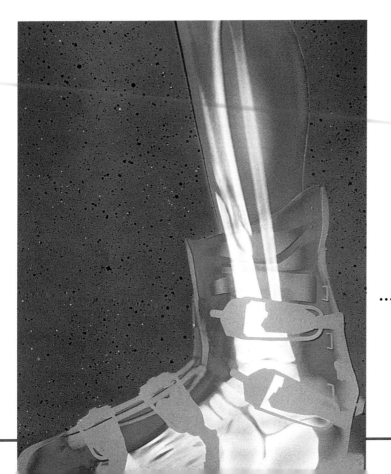

An X ray reveals the tell-tale signs of a sports injury. Here, a skier's lower leg has been broken in a serious fall.

Knee and elbow joints work like hinges, or simple levers. Shoulder and hip joints are examples of ball-and-socket joints. The ball-like end of the arm bone, called the humerus, fits into a socketlike hole in the shoulder blade, or scapula. These joints can sometimes dislocate. When a rugby player falls awkwardly after a tackle, a shoulder may dislocate. The "ball" literally comes out of the "socket." A physiotherapist can usually put a dislocated shoulder back in position.

Muscle Wear and Tear

A sharp blow to a muscle may burst a blood vessel. When this happens, blood collects in the muscle and clots. This causes a bruise, which makes movement painful. Pulled muscles usually include damage to a **tendon.** If you have a torn Achilles tendon (which attaches the calf muscle to your heel bone), you will probably have to walk with crutches for several months while the damage heals.

Despite heavy protective clothing, football players are likely to suffer from injuries at some point in their careers.

A BODY AT WORK

Your heart beats about 70 times a minute. That is nearly 37 million times each year! Your heart is made of a special kind of muscle that works without tiring. A healthy person is unaware that these muscles are working. And the same is true of those muscles involved in breathing. The muscles you use to move your arms and legs are called skeletal muscles. Like your heart muscle, they need energy to work properly. Working out helps you to use the energy you get from your food more effectively. How do your muscles, lungs, and heart work together?

Fit Test

The Harvard step test is one way to find out how fit you are. You step up and down every two seconds for five minutes. The step should be about 20 inches high. After resting for one minute, you check your pulse (your heart beat) for 30 seconds. After a 30-second pause, you check your pulse again and, after another 30-second pause, once more. If you are fit, your heart rate should slow down and go back to its normal rate quickly after exercise. If your heart rate takes a long time to slow down, then you are not as fit as you could be. The resting heart rate of an athlete may be only 30 beats a minute, because the athlete's blood circulation has improved as a result of fitness training. Tiny blood vessels can enlarge by as much as five times during exercise. Blood circulation is boosted at the start of a race when a hormone (body chemical) called adrenaline speeds up an athlete's heart rate. It rushes into the bloodstream, making the athlete's heart rate reach around 200 beats a minute.

....

"Step" exercises are great fun. They are also a superb way to increase fitness and develop a healthy heart.

A Breath of Air

How does the oxygen in the air reach your blood? You have tiny air sacs called alveoli in your lungs. They are surrounded by tiny blood vessels. It is here that oxygen passes from your lungs into your blood. The more fit you are, the more efficiently your lungs work, and the more oxygen they take from the air each time you breathe.

The Importance of Training

To be fit you need to have endurance, flexibility, speed, and strength. Each sport demands a different training program that focuses on a particular area of fitness. A swimmer, for example, must have endurance; sprinters need speed; a weightlifter, above all, needs strength, and gymnasts need flexibility.

Oxygen passes into the blood. Air sacs called alveoli collect air from the lungs and send oxygen to the blood vessels around them.

BURNING IT UP

Do you know how much energy is in the different foods you eat? You can find out by looking at the labels on packaged foods, which give the amount of energy per serving of food. A candy bar has 230 calories and an egg about 75 calories. The energy you get from food is released in your muscles whenever you move. A football player, for example, might burn up 540 calories in an hour.

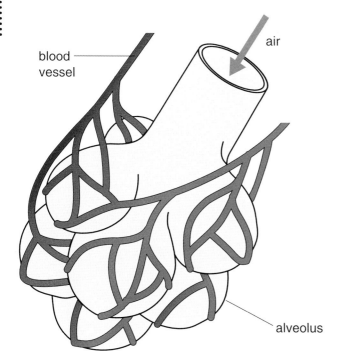

blood vessel

air

alveolus

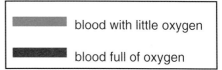

blood with little oxygen

blood full of oxygen

THE SCORE

Think about two sports in which the score is kept in different ways. In a figure-skating competition, the score for a skater may be 7.8. This is an average of all the scores from the judges. Each judge decides separately how well the skater performed, and some award a higher score than others. The score in a soccer game is different. A result of 3–2 clearly means that the team that scored 3 goals has won. The results in many other sports, such as track and javelin throwing, depend on precise measurement. How do scorekeepers make sure that these measurements are accurate?

Timekeepers

In most school and amateur athletic competitions, the timekeepers use stopwatches. They wait by the finishing line with their finger on a button. When the starter's pistol fires, they press a button to start the stopwatch. They wait by the finishing line and as the winner crosses the tape they stop the watch. It takes about 10 seconds to run 100 yards. If there is more than one timekeeper, the times of the different timekeepers are averaged. Clearly an error of 0.1 seconds makes a huge difference when there may be a difference of only 0.01 seconds separating the first and second place runners. Now compare this to a 10,000-yard race (which takes about 30 minutes) The same error of 0.1 seconds is much less important. At major sporting events, the timing is entirely electronic. The electronic clock starts automatically as the starting pistol fires.

Electronic scoreboards and giant video screens are just two of the developments that have changed the way we watch and enjoy sporting events.

Reaction Time

Everyone has a reaction time. This is the time it takes, for example, for an athlete to hear a starting pistol and to start running. The reaction time is generally not much more than 0.1 seconds. A race car driver might have a reaction time of about 0.2 seconds. The reaction time of a timekeeper operating a stopwatch or of a line-court judge in a tennis match, may well change the result of a race or a match!

In or Out?

Electronic equipment is also used in sports like tennis. In tennis, this equipment helps judges decide whether the ball is good, or "in bounds." As it leaves the server's racket, the ball can travel more than 120 miles per hour. At this speed, there is often a difference of opinion between the player and the line-court judge. An electronic eye can "see" exactly where the ball lands. It beeps loudly to signal that the ball is out.

"ON YOUR MARKS"

When starting pistols were first used in athletic competitions, timekeepers started their watches when they heard the bang. But sound takes 0.3 seconds to travel 328 feet! Now timekeepers start their watches when they see the smoke from the pistol, because light travels at 186,282 miles per second.

The race is over, but the work has just begun for the judges who have to decide the winner.

27

TELEVISED SPORTS

Watching sports has always been a popular pastime. And today television allows many people to watch one event, as it happens. For example, television made it possible for 33.4 million people to watch the 1993 Superbowl. This was a record for a single program. Now some major events can only be seen on satellite television, unless you are actually in the audience at the event! Television, together with telephoto camera lenses and slow-motion photography, have changed the way we watch sports.

BILLIONS OF VIEWERS

In 1990, 26.5 billion TV viewers watched the 1990 soccer World Cup finals.

Close-up Work

When you use a magnifying glass, you hold it a certain distance from the object to focus the image. A camera lens focuses in the same way. The distance for an ordinary 35-millimeter camera lens is about 2 inches. This is called the focal length. A telephoto lens can focus at four times that distance (8 inches). Such lenses are like short telescopes, because everything you see through them looks much closer than it really is.

The photo below was taken with a zoom lens, a telephoto lens with a focal length that can be changed to make the image fill the frame. Skilled camera operators can use these lenses to follow the leader in a race or a play at the goal.

Slow Motion

Was it a goal? Which horse finished first? Was that serve out? These are the questions often asked in sports. The TV viewer can often see the play in question again and again—and in slow motion. How? A normal movie film is made by taking 24 separate pictures every second. You do not see the pictures separately, because your eyes keep seeing something after it is no longer in front of them. This is called **persistence of vision.** Your eyes take time to adjust to each new picture. If you look at a film played at half-speed, then the action also slows down to half-speed. This is slow motion.

Pictures Around the World

Communications satellites circle the earth at the same speed as the earth's rotation. This allows them to stay over the same area of the globe at all times. Radio and television signals, which can only travel in straight lines, are beamed up by a satellite dish in one country to the nearest communications satellite in space. It boosts the signal, using energy from its solar panels. The signal is then beamed back to a satellite dish in another country. In this way, a football game can be seen on TV all around the world as it is being played.

Television networks are always finding new ways to get viewers closer to the action. Cameras on rails can follow every move of a soccer player as he runs up the field.

GLOSSARY

aluminum a very light strong metal

carbon fiber a very pure and fine fiber made of carbon. It is used to make plastic materials strong.

cartilage the soft tissue where bones meet. The same kind of tissue also supports the ears, nose, and larynx (voice box).

compress squeeze something together so that it takes up a smaller space

elastic something that returns to its normal shape by itself after being stretched or squashed

fiberglass strong plastic material reinforced with matting made from finely spun glass fibers, sometimes called GRP or glass reinforced plastic

free-fall fall freely through the atmosphere, usually before a parachute opens

friction the force between two surfaces rubbing together, which slows their movement and produces heat

gear wheel a wheel with "teeth" spaced regularly around its rim

isotonic drink solution of chemical substances adjusted not to disturb the chemical balance of substances in a person's body

Kevlar an artificial material so strong that it can be used in bullet-proof vests or twisted into cables stronger than steel

kinetic energy the energy a moving body has because it is moving

mechanical advantage the amount by which your effort is multiplied, for example, by a car jack that enables you to lift up the car

microchip a complete electronic circuit built on a small piece of silicon, used in computers, cars, radios, televisions, etc.

molecule the smallest amount of a substance that can exist by itself and still have all the same properties as the substance

momentum the force something gains by its motion

persistence of vision when the eye continues to see an object in the same place after it has moved a little

polymer a chemical substance made by joining together many repeating units of a simpler chemical substance. It can occur in nature or be artificial.

reaction time the time it takes for the body to react after it has seen something; for example, the amount of time it takes to apply the brakes of a car after seeing a dog run across the road

slalom a ski race down a zig-zag course marked out by flag poles

tendon the strand of very strong tissue that connects a muscle to a bone

turbulence the irregular flow of air or fluid around something

FACT FILE

- In 1980 there were four left-handers among the top 10 tennis players. At the world table-tennis championships, there were six left-handers among the top 10. Some people believe that left-handers have a quicker reflex than right-handers. This "leftie advantage" seems to be useful in fencing, boxing, squash, and cricket, as well as tennis. However, not all experts agree.

- Some athletes imagine themselves playing their sport before actually competing. This is called visualization. Javelin throwers, for example, might imagine themselves making a perfect throw. Baseball players might imagine hitting homeruns. Why all this make believe? Because when it comes to really performing, athletes who use visualization are likely to perform better because they believe they can do better.

- Modern chemical techniques are used to detect tiny amounts of drugs in athletes. Some athletes take drugs to build their muscles and increase their endurance. Athletes are regularly tested. This can be done easily with a urine sample, which is analyzed in a laboratory. Very accurate instruments are used to identify any unusual substance in the urine.

- Many records would be smashed in an athletic competition on the moon. The moon's gravity is six times weaker than the gravity on earth. So there is less pulling force to keep things, including people, on the surface of the moon. High-jumpers would do pretty well on the moon! And a shot-putter could make a throw that would truly go out of this world!

FURTHER READINGS

Everst, James. *Name Your Adventure: Sports.* Alladin. 1995.

Gardner, Robert. *Experimenting with Science in Sports.* Franklin Watts, 1993.

Isberg, Emily. *Peak Performance.* Simon & Schuster, 1989.

INDEX